Thank you Dad for always bringing laughter and joy to my life.

Some dads love to watch TV,
To bake or play the flute.
But my dad's into something else,
Yes, my dad loves to toot.

TOOT!

He toots all day when he's awake,
And all night when he's sleeping.
And once, when he was hard at work,
He tooted in a meeting.

He loves to toot so very much,
He makes up tooting games.
He also calls his tooting sounds
A bunch of silly names.

His toots have many silly names:
Trouser Coughs and *Trumps*,
Botty Burps and *Panty Pops*,
And *Huffy Guffs* and *Pumps!*

Official
Tooty Nicknames

Trouser Coughs

Trumps

Botty Burps

Panty Pops

Huffy Guffs

Pumps

The problem is Dad toots so often,
He gets into trouble.
And since he likes to toot so much,
Not tooting is a struggle.

His favorite game is *Tooty Noise,*

Where the loudest toot's the winner.

My mother never looks amused
When he plays it during dinner.

Once when he was at the store, his toot, it made a whiff.

He thought he'd got away with it, until he took a sniff.

The lady next to him in line
Was the first person to notice,
And as the smell filled up the store,
It killed all of the roses.

From wall to wall, the toot smell spread
At quite an alarming rate.
In fact, it was so bad
They had to evacuate!

Then there was this other time when Dad went to the library,
Where the only rule to know is that you must be reading quietly.

He was starting chapter two
Of a book on bathroom plumbing.
When deep inside, he felt a growl.
A brand-new toot was coming.

The toot, it echoed 'round the room
And made the readers stare.

Such a strong toot it was,
Dad shot up in the air!

Dad was quite embarrassed
So he made his exit fast.
But he didn't learn his lesson,
For that toot was not his last.

And you can't forget the *Parents' Race*
At my school field day.
Oh that was when Dad's tooting
Really put him on display.

Dad was up in second place
And nearly at the end

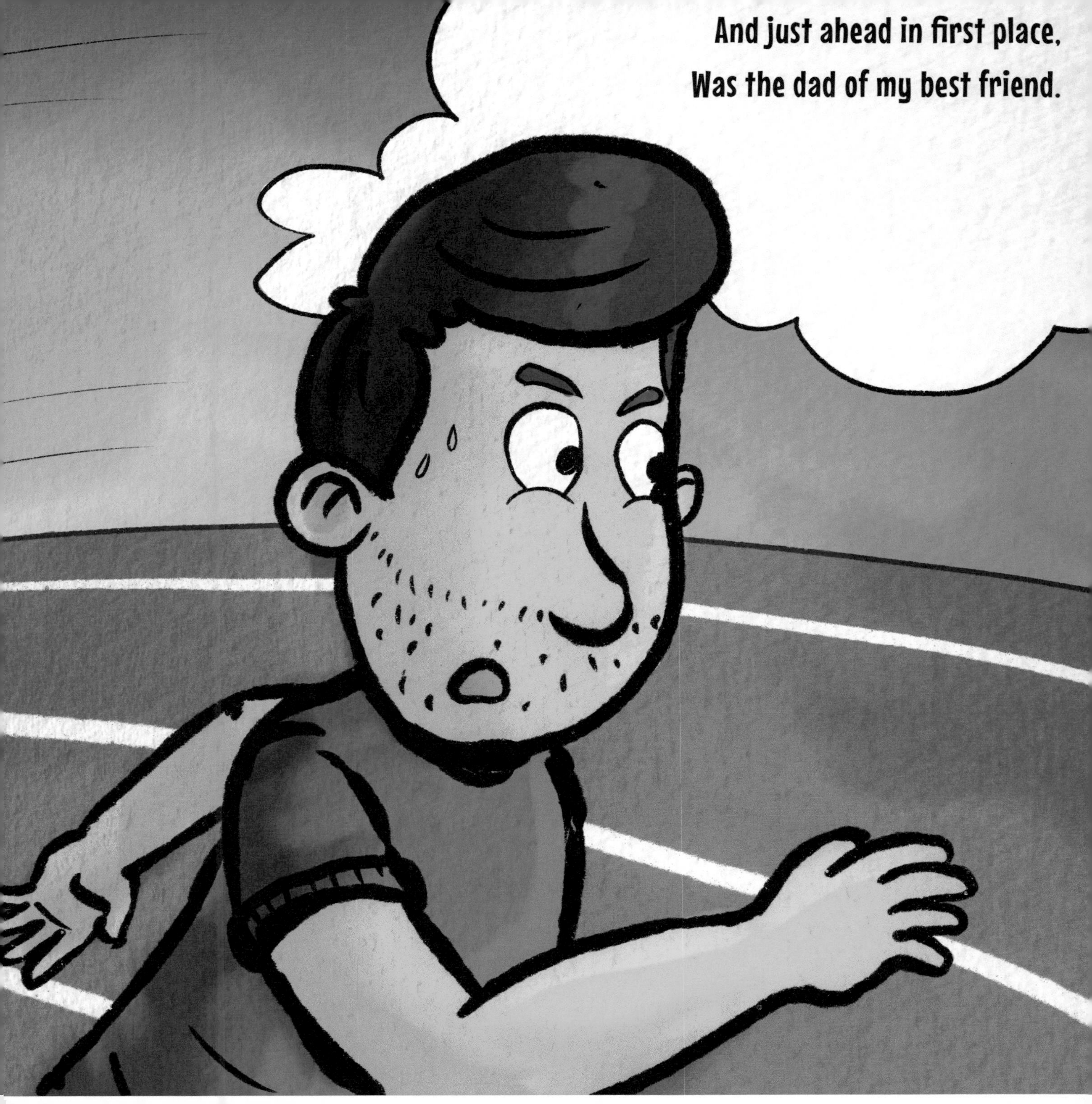
And just ahead in first place,
Was the dad of my best friend.

Dad had to find a way
To get himself ahead.
Instead of running harder though,
He tooted hard instead.

With the help of his rocket toot,
He crossed the finish line,
And overtook my best friend's dad
In just the nick of time.

The crowd, they cheered and clapped
When Dad shot past the man.

Thanks to his big 'Rocket Fart',
Dad's race had gone to plan.

It was so fun, to see for once,
Dad's tooting paying off.

I was proud of Dad that day
And his winning botty cough.

After the commotion,
Of that race winning day,

I hugged my Dad tightly,
And had these words to say...

"You're my hero Dad.
I love it when you toot!"

"One day I too will be like you,
And learn to play the trouser flute!"

Dear reader,

Thank you so much for purchasing and reading this book. It would mean the world to me as an author if you shared your impressions. Please take two minutes to share your review on Amazon with the millions of parents and children (and me!) who are waiting for your valued feedback.

Yours truly,
Tom

Made in the USA
Columbia, SC
18 November 2023

26672861R00022